Stars Are Silver

and other short stories

Very Large Print

Stefania Hartley

THE*SICILIAN*MAMA

ALSO AVAILABLE AS EBOOK
AND SMALLER FONT
PAPERBACK

ISBN: 978-1-914606-08-3

All these stories were first
published in The People's
Friend magazine.

Cover photo from Canva

To my very own Tanino and Melina, with much love. xxx

CONTENTS

1. MUSIC FROM ABOVE

When someone asked Filomena Gattuso why she was still single— you'd be surprised how many people asked this kind of questions in Sicily—she always replied with the proverb, "Better alone than in bad company". She was happy on her own, thank you very much.

In truth, she had waited sixty-three years for "The One" to turn up on her doorstep, but he never had. She had judiciously swept that doorstep of other suitors and had kept it gleaming and sparkling all these years, but her soulmate hadn't even passed by.

By now she had concluded that something most dreadful must have happened to him. He could have accidentally decapitated himself while shaving. He might have lost life and limb in a naval accident while on a cruise. Or, more disappointingly, he could have been snatched by another woman.

This particular thought irked Filomena so much that sometimes she forced herself to imagine different scenarios, in which missing each other in life had been her fault instead. He could have been waiting for her at that school where she never took up the post they offered her, or at the Chopin concert in 1999 that she missed because she had a bad cold.

Filomena unhooked her shopping trolley from the wall, checked herself in the mirror and adjusted the collar of her coat. She closed the door of her flat and called the lift down.

The condominium's entrance lobby was simmering with people: clients of the doctors and solicitors who practised in the building, fellow residents going about their daily business, builders and handymen with their tools— everyone was there.

"*Buongiorno*, good morning, Pietro. Any post for me?" Filomena asked the porter.

The man scrunched his face into an apology. "I'm sorry, I haven't sorted it yet. It's chaos here today," he said, pointing to the lorry parked by the entrance.

"Who's moving out?"

"In. They're moving into the flat above yours."

Filomena didn't like the sound of that. The previous occupants, a family of five, wore wooden clogs and played basketball indoors.

"Do you know who? Is it a family?" Do they wear soft slippers, she thought but didn't ask.

"It's a man on his own," Pietro said, then leaped out of his seat, shouting to the removal lorry. "You've got to leave space for people to get in and out!"

A woman was trying to fit her twin stroller through the gap between the lorry and the entrance doors. Filomena walked up to them.

"Park at the back where the garages are," the porter shouted at the large man in the lorry's cab.

"Do you want me to shove a piano into the kitchen? The sitting-room is on this side," the man retorted, gesticulating towards the sky.

A piano. That should be more pleasant than wooden clogs,

Filomena thought. She stepped through the gap and looked up curiously.

A beautiful grand piano dangled off a crane, tied around the middle with thick ropes. It reminded her of the way children carry cats by their belly, and it didn't look right. It looked so not right that, when it started tilting to one side, Filomena could already see it falling. On her.

One rope slipped, then another, and the piano escaped the crane's clutches like a cat leaping out of a child's arms.

Filomena froze to the spot. Her

life flashed before her. All the love she had given, would have liked to give, and that which she had received—plus a hefty helping of a much less noble sentiment towards the owner of the piano—exploded in her chest.

The next thing she knew was that she was flat on the pavement. The sound of cracking wood and tinkling strings filled the air. Through the ground, the shockwaves rippled through her body.

I must be dead.

She opened her eyes and saw a

pair of arms wrapped around her. They wore a dark green corduroy jacket and a dusting of black hair on the back of the hands. They were certainly not hers.

The arms slipped off her waist, hitched her under her armpits and tugged her up, the way a child pulls another child off the floor. Confused, she slowly turned around. The arms that had pulled her up now had a body, a face and a pair of warm brown eyes.

"Are you alright?" the man asked. Wrinkles of worry creased his brow. He had thick salt-and-pepper hair, long dark eyelashes and a handsome moustache.

A frisson of something new and very pleasant ran through Filomena's body. This man had saved her life and there was no ring on his ring finger. Maybe, in her near-death experience, the clock of her life had been wound back to the moment when she was due to meet The One.

"I've never been better," she answered.

He let out a sigh of relief and offered her his hand. "I'm Dario. I'm sorry about pushing you to the ground, but I guessed that the alternative would have been worse." He glanced at the piano's wreck still billowing dust. "Can I get you anything? A chair or a glass of water?"

As a caring smile stretched across his face, Filomena felt warmed from the inside. "No, really. I'm fine."

"Great. Well, I'd better go and check on my piano."

My piano? The man went from hero to villain in less than one second and Filomena's heart dropped. Her handsome saviour was actually her murderer.

***

Filomena stared at the cup of coffee that Gabriella, the porter's wife, had put in front of her.

"Poor you. What a scare you must have got. It's a miracle that you haven't broken anything! Drink your coffee and your water," she said, offering her also a glass of water and a biscuit from a tin.

"Things like this make you think how precarious life is. One moment we're pulling our trolley to the supermarket, the next we're pulled in a trolley and boxed into a coffin," Filomena said. Out of the corner of her eye she saw Gabriella touch the metals legs of the table, in the typical Sicilian way of touching iron to stave off bad luck.

"You're right. We should enjoy every moment we have," Gabriella said, taking another couple of biscuits from the tin and popping one into her mouth.

"Quite. Was it Horace, the Latin poet, who said '*carpe diem*', seize the day?"

Gabriella gave her a blank look. "I thought it was my idea."

"Whoever said it first, it's a jolly

good idea."

When her life had flashed before her eyes under the falling piano, her only regret had been not to have found The One. Could he still be out at large? If not, did he have a substitute—an "Another One"?

"I'd better get going," she said, standing up.

"But you haven't even touched your coffee."

"Sorry, I have to go, I haven't got much time."

"The supermarket doesn't shut till eight o'clock."

Filomena gave Gabriella a

puzzled look. "I'm not going to the supermarket. I'm going to get myself a date."

***

The first thing she did was to dig out her list of attributes of The One. It was pencilled on a cutting from a women's magazine entitled 'How to Choose a Man'. The magazine gave ten bullet points, but Filomena had added thirty more of her own.

Now that she was looking for "Another One", the list needed revisiting. She struck off points that had once been deal-breakers and, after a while, she tore the whole thing up. No list this time.

***

Dario hadn't bought flowers since his wife's funeral, but he felt that he should give his new neighbour some to say sorry about the piano incident.

It wasn't a romantic gift. Not at all. Even though he had felt a flutter of something in his chest when he had held her close—it must be normal to experience heightened senses in situations of danger. He was only buying flowers to say sorry.

"How can I help you?" the florist asked.

"I'd like a bunch of flowers."

"What kind?"

"I don't know. They're for a woman, to say sorry."

The florist wiped a hand on her apron and darted him a suspicious and unsympathetic glance. "How much do you need to spend?"

Dario noticed that she had said 'need' rather than 'wish'. "How much do you suggest?"

She cocked an eyebrow. "It depends on how sorry you need to be."

"Very," he said.

The woman clicked her tongue and completely emptied the container of red roses.

Dario returned home with a bunch of thirty-seven scarlet roses. He wrote a card, prepared his apology speech and walked downstairs to the flat below.

But there was no answer to the doorbell. So he fetched a vase from his apartment and put the roses in front of his neighbour's door, along with the card and his hope.

***

Filomena had enjoyed her evening out with Matteo from the Purchasing Department. She enjoyed evenings out and she didn't get enough of them. It had been flattering to receive a bouquet of freesias, too, especially as she wasn't used to being the object of male attention.

But she had never considered her colleague The One, and that night was no exception. She disagreed with most of his opinions, disliked the way he slurped his drinks when she had lunch with him in the work canteen, and was disgusted by the food still stuck in his unkempt moustache when he left the office at one minute to five. However, her standards for Another One were not as high as for The One, so all in all Matteo could do the job.

"I'll come up to your door. You never know who could be lurking in the stairwell."

"I've never had any problems before, and this is a very respectable condominium," she replied, but he insisted.

Filomena couldn't believe it when

the lift reached her floor and she saw an enormous bunch of red roses sitting in a crystal vase in front of her door.

"It looks like you have a secret admirer, Filomena." Matteo's eyes darted from the gargantuan bunch of red roses to the tiny bouquet of freesia in her hands.

"I have no admirers. I have no idea who they're from."

"We'll find out soon enough," Matteo said, snatching up a little white envelope and opening it without waiting for permission. "*Sorry about earlier. Dario*," he read aloud, then raised an eyebrow. "A not-so-secret admirer, then. Who could have known that our Filomena was such a heartbreaker?" he said caustically.

Matteo barely said goodbye before disappearing into the lift without even a glance or a wave through the little glass window. Filomena immediately realised that she was going to have to find herself another Another One.

But she had a more immediate problem: the crystal vase holding her roses looked like something her neighbour had grabbed from his flat to prop up the bunch rather than as part of the gift. At some point, she would have to return it. To the man who had almost killed her with his piano.

***

Filomena's next date was Girolamo. They had been at school together and Facebook certified that he was still single.

"I'll never forget how you helped me with that maths homework. Do you remember?" she told him as soon as they met outside Palermo's opera house, both half an hour early to their rendezvous.

That immediately broke the ice because Girolamo didn't just remember the topic of that homework, but even the solution. It was a promising start for a date.

Girolamo had aged better than other men and didn't sit on the lowest ranks of the male beauty scale anymore but hovered comfortably around the middle. By the time the violins were tuning up, Filomena was convinced that she could soon switch her Facebook status from Single to In A Relationship.

The concert began and the music

immediately enraptured her, especially the piano. It sang with all the emotions of a human voice and brought Filomena to tears. Never had a concert been so moving. She turned to Girolamo, convinced that he'd be in tears, too, and instead found him asleep.

Who was this wonderful pianist? Before a concert, she usually read all about the performers, but this time she had been too busy reading about Girolamo on Facebook.

At the interval, she managed to get hold of a programme, and her jaw slackened when a familiar face smiled at her from the cover: her new neighbour! Filomena went straight for the biography.

'Dario Ben Jelloun. Born in Palermo to Moroccan parents, his extraordinary talent was discovered by his primary school teacher who put him forward for the prestigious Tchaikovsky bursary which allowed him to study at the conservatoire despite his family's financial difficulties.'

She imagined it going on: *He now lives above the flat of Filomena Gattuso, whom he saved from a falling piano last week.*

Her new neighbour, the one who had wrapped his arms around her and saved her life, was the pianist that played like an angel. As the concert resumed, Filomena's heart fluttered at every trill of the piano, and Girolamo's chances fell faster than the decrescendo at the end of the last sonata.

***

The doorbell rang at 11.00 am. It wasn't too early, but Dario always granted himself a little lie-in after a concert.

He dragged himself out of bed

and padded to the door. When he looked through the peephole, his heart did a somersault. Even distorted by the lens, his neighbour was still beautiful. Panic seized him. She was in her Sunday best— it was Sunday, after all—while he was in pyjamas.

"One moment, please!" he called through the door.

He grabbed the trench coat hanging on the coat stand and put it over his pyjamas, then checked himself in the mirror and decided that a hat was required, too. Finally, he opened the door.

"I wanted to say thank you for the roses," she said, looking even lovelier than the first time he'd seen her. "Here is your vase," she added, handing him his crystal vase.

He reached out and their fingers brushed, giving him goose bumps.

"My pleasure."

"I was at your concert last night. You play wonderfully. I was moved."

He felt his cheeks heat up and didn't know where to rest his gaze, so he looked down at his feet, still clad in slippers below his pyjama bottoms. "Thank you."

"Well, I seem to have interrupted you while you were going out," she remarked, looking at his hat and coat. "I'd better leave you in peace."

***

Filomena knew immediately when Dario got his new piano. The music rang loud and clear through her ceiling.

She experimented with ways to hear it better. Keeping the windows open helped a lot, as did sitting on the balcony, and even standing just below her metal chandelier. The one thing that made all the difference, though, was whether or not he had his window open. Then it was like being in the same room.

Sometimes she fantasized about ringing his doorbell and asking to sit in the room with him, but he'd probably think that she was trying to scrounge a concert without paying.

She also fantasized about passing him on the stairs or in the lobby, but he spent most of his time at home playing. Listening to his music for Filomena became like listening to his voice.

***

It was his wife's anniversary and, like every year, Dario couldn't play. But he had a concert coming up so he forced himself to sit at the piano and work at the piece until his fingers hurt.

He toiled and laboured until dinner time, when he found no food in the cupboard or in the fridge. He would have to go out and buy something.

He combed his hair and checked himself in the mirror—there was always a chance he could meet his neighbour.

That day, as he came out of the lift on the ground floor, she was there.

"I'm glad you're going out. You've been working very hard today," she said with a kind smile that shot straight at his heart.

"You hear me?" Of course she would, as his flat wasn't soundproof, but he had never thought about it before.

"I do. I love it, especially when you keep your windows open. Then I feel like I'm in the room."

"You can be in the room!" he

exclaimed before he had had a chance to overthink it. "Come up now and I'll play for you."

"Oh, that's very kind, but I wouldn't want you to change your plans," she replied.

"I was only going to buy some dinner, but I can do it later," he quickly assured her.

"I have an idea." She smiled. "Why don't we have dinner at mine, then we go up to yours for some music?"

Dario though that she was the cleverest person on earth and her idea was pure genius.

"Marvellous."

That was the first of many dinners and many lunches together.

Eventually, they knocked a hole in the floor and built a spiral staircase to join their flats and their lives.

Sometimes Dario marvelled at how lucky he had been to find love and happiness for a second time in his life.

"I can't believe that I found you single," he said to Filomena one day.

She smiled. "Of course you did.

I've been waiting for you all these years. Were you playing at the Chopin concert in May 1999?"

Even after all that time, he knew the answer, because that was the concert where he had met his first wife. "Yes, I was."

Filomena smiled and let out a breath. "I finally know who's to blame. Not you. Not me. Just a silly bout of the cold!"

2. LIKE A NEW WOMAN

Melina loved going to her hairdresser. Carmen was always the first to know about weddings, funerals and new jobs, and Melina enjoyed being filled in with all the latest news.

She felt pampered when Carmen

washed, combed and styled her hair, and she loved a little chat.

That day, Melina walked into the salon and found Carmen spreading hair dye on her friend Peppina's head.

"I am sorry, Melina, you will have to wait. Peppina's colour is taking longer than I had planned," Carmen apologised.

Melina didn't mind waiting, but she hated the feeling of being last in the pecking order. That usually happened because she didn't get big jobs done to her hair, like perms or colour.

"Peppina, it's always you," Melina teased her friend, sitting on the empty chair next to her. "I bet that you couldn't make up your mind about what colour you wanted on your head."

"Oh, Melina, please, don't vex me. You have no idea how much I suffer. I wish I could leave my hair white like yours, but Rocco insists that I colour it."

"Rocco? What does your husband care about it?" Melina asked her, incredulous.

"He cares a lot, and he didn't like the colour I had last time, so

Carmen and I have had to choose a new one just now."

"Next time, I'll give you the colour samples to take home and you can show them to your husband first," Carmen suggested.

Melina couldn't imagine getting Tanino interested in hair colour samples. "Tanino doesn't even notice when I have my hair cut."

"Lucky you!" Peppina exclaimed.

"Of course he doesn't, Melina. You never have anything more drastic than a couple of centimetres taken off the length," Carmen reminded her. "I'm sure that he would notice if you went home with, say, a different colour," she added, slathering colouring cream on Peppina's head.

"If he didn't, he'd either be blind or he'd be going out with another woman," Peppina put in.

That thought made Melina shudder. What if Tanino wasn't interested in the way she looked because he had another woman? There was only one way to find out.

Melina straightened on her chair. "I want my hair coloured, Carmen," she declared.

"Oh. When?"

"Now."

"Now? Don't you want to go home and discuss it with your husb—"

"No. I want my hair coloured as soon as you finish with Peppina. If you haven't got enough time for the haircut, too, I will do without the cut this time."

"OK. If you are sure, then here is the sampler. Choose the colour." Carmen handed her a wheel with tufts of coloured plastic hair and numbers.

Melina's eyes were immediately

drawn to the brightest and boldest colours.

"This is the colour you were before you went white," Peppina said, pointing to a dark brown.

"I don't like it."

How was Tanino ever going to notice if she went for the same colour she had been before? *If he doesn't notice, he's either blind or he's got another woman.* Tanino must notice. Melina pointed her finger straight to the flame red. "I want this one."

"Wow, that's a change," Carmen replied. "Your husband will love it or hate it. You should show the sample to him and come back tomorrow."

"No. I want this. I want it now."

***

Tanino was worried: Melina should have been home by now. But when she walked through the door, he became even more worried. What had she done to her hair? Until that morning she'd had lovely white hair. Now she was as red as a chilli pepper!

Had he never told her that he loved her snow-white hair? Perhaps not. Too late now. If you can't say anything good, don't say anything at all, his mother had taught him. So Tanino decided not to say a word about Melina's new hair.

"Sorry I'm late."

Usually he would have asked her where she had been. On this unfortunate occasion, it was terribly obvious. "It's okay, dear."

"When I realised that I was going to be late for lunch, I bought some pizza from the baker." Melina opened the parcel and put the two pizza slices on their plates. The tomato sauce looked much the same colour as her hair. "Do you prefer—"

"Not at all!" he interrupted.

"— the pizza with the anchovies or the one without?" she continued with a frown.

"Ah. Anchovies, please."

They sat down and ate in silence. What could they possibly talk about without mentioning the elephant in the room?

Every now and then, Tanino felt Melina's gaze dart to him, but he carefully avoided it. He had no idea what he should he say if she asked him how he liked her new hair. If he lied, she would keep it. If he told her the truth, she could he hurt.

As soon as they'd finished eating, he scuttled out of the room and turned on the TV.

***

"He hasn't noticed, Anna. My hair is bright red, like a flaming fire, and he hasn't said a word!" Melina whispered on the phone to her friend. "Do you think that he doesn't care about me anymore? Do you think that Peppina is right and that he does have another woman?"

"Don't listen to Peppina!" Anna

replied. "Some men have selective blindness to their wives' hair. Maybe they dread to think how much the hairdresser cost, so they just don't want to know. But he'll surely notice if you change the way you dress. Try that."

"I never wear trousers. I could buy a pair of trousers."

"Good idea! Let's go shopping together."

***

Melina was late again for supper. Tanino filled a pot with water and put it on the hob. He didn't fancy two takeaway meals in a row. If she found a pot of bubbling water, she might take the hint and cook him some pasta.

But the water boiled and he had to turn the hob off twice before Melina got home.

As well as her hideous hair, now she had a pair of hideous jeans. What had happened to his lovely wife? A frightening thought bolted through his mind: was she trying to impress another man? Did she have a lover? Tanino felt dizzy and had to sit down.

"Hello dear." She stopped on the kitchen threshold as if expecting him to say something.

Or was she about to tell him about the other man?

Tanino shot to his feet and made himself busy at the stove, turning his back to her. He didn't want to have that conversation. Not now, not ever. He wanted everything to stay the same. He and his Melina, together eating pasta with tomato sauce, day after day. He poured the pasta in the water and accidentally the packet, too.

"I'm sorry I'm late."

"It's OK." He was never going to ask where she had been, why she was wearing jeans and who had bought them for her.

She walked around the table and planted herself right next to him, one jeans-clad leg forward. He looked away.

"I bought a roast chicken from the shop when I realised that I was going to be late," she said, putting a takeaway parcel on the counter, "but I see that you're already cooking some pasta."

"I don't mind. Chicken is fine. Whatever you like, my dear." He picked up the pot and poured water, pasta and packet into the sink.

"Are you OK, dear?" she asked.

"Me? Yes, of course. Are *you* OK?"

"More than OK. I'm feeling like a new woman." She looked at him suggestively.

That was it. At that moment Tanino had no doubt that his beloved wife of 50 years had a new man.

***

"He hasn't noticed the jeans, either, Anna. I even stuck my leg out in front of him! Not a comment—nothing—as if I were invisible. He has another woman, hasn't he?" Melina was in despair.

"I'm sorry, Melina," Anna replied.

"Oh, Anna, what will I do?"

"Move to the sofa. If he's guilty, he'll think that you've found him out and will confess. If he's not guilty, he'll finally pay attention to you."

Melina took her pillow, a spare blanket, her reading glasses and her book, and made herself cosy on the sofa.

On his way back from the bathroom to their bedroom, Tanino saw her from the corridor. His eyes became coffee saucers and his face blanched. "What on earth? Are you sleeping here?"

"Yes. Why? Did you want to watch the TV here?" she asked.

"Heavens, no! Look, Melina, if there's something that you need to tell me, tell me clearly. At lunchtime you came home with shocking red hair, at dinnertime you turned up in jeans, and now you move out of our bedroom. What am I to think? I'm only a man, I can't guess. If I try, the things I imagine are so horrible that I want to believe that they're not true. Please, tell me what's going on."

"You noticed my hair?"

"Yes, and I didn't like it a bit."

"And you noticed my jeans?"

"Yes, and I liked them even less. I want my lovely wife back. I want my sweet Melina." He was almost shaking.

Melina leapt off the sofa and wrapped her arms around him. "You did notice! You do care about me! You don't have a new woman!" she cried.

"Melina, keeping up with you is such hard work that I would never have the energy to run after anyone else."

She kissed him. "That's all I needed to hear, because you don't need to. You can have your old Melina back. I'm returning the jeans and I'm going back to my hairdresser tomorrow!"

True to her words, the next day Melina went straight back to Carmen's salon—and this time she was given emergency status and top priority to have her hair dyed back to white!

3. PERICLE'S PROMISE

"Gatecrash a wedding?"

"So long as we don't eat their food, what harm can we do?" Greta replied to her daughter.

"Intrude on their privacy," Melanie shot back, her knuckles white around the steering wheel of their hire car. "We can't turn up at a wedding just because we've seen white balloons on a lamppost."

"If this venue is available, we need to know. We're running out of time," Greta argued. It was only two weeks to Melanie's wedding and they had come from London to this remote part of the Sicilian countryside for a final check on the reception venue. Instead, they'd been told their booking had been cancelled because of urgent building works.

"Unless you want to postpone the wedding, sweetheart?" Greta asked.

"Impossible, Mum. Everything is arranged. The guests have booked their flights and hotel. We just need a venue for the reception that's not too far from the church. I'm sure we can find a venue nearby, but maybe not in two days. Would you be OK with staying another week or two?"

That was the question Greta dreaded. She had a photoshoot in London on Monday morning. She hadn't told her daughter that. Melanie believed that her mother continued to model at seventy-four out of nothing but vanity. She didn't know that Greta couldn't afford to stop working.

"Let's just see what we find in this villa before changing any plans," she replied.

Through a cloud of pink and white almond blossom emerged a grand baroque villa. The façade was clad in wisteria, and the purple blossoms dangled like the fringes of a flapper dress. A graceful double staircase opened in front of them like an embrace. Melanie pulled into the busy car park.

"I really like this place."

The music of a piano wafted out of the open French windows and the air was rich with the scent of the wisteria. They followed the notes of the piano up the grand staircase, through stuccoed corridors, and stopped on the threshold of a magnificent ballroom.

In the centre of the room, surrounded by the guests' tables, was a grand piano perched on a platform. But it was the pianist himself that captured Greta's attention.

He was about her age, with jade

eyes framed by dark eyebrows and an elegantly trimmed white beard. He looked refined without affectation, and his body swayed with the melody, as if an extension of the piano. It was a melody Greta had heard before, though never played with such emotion.

***

The last time Pericle had touched the keys of a piano it had been for Laura. When his fiancée had closed her eyes for the last time, his music had died with her.

But the string quartet the bride and groom had booked had failed to turn up and, of course, he had stepped in.

Hosting weddings wasn't just a job for Pericle. It was a calling, and he cared about every couple as if they were his own children.

Every wedding was as important as if it was his own—the wedding with Laura that had never happened. Now those notes brought back memories as vivid as if they had happened 50 minutes rather than 50 years ago.

Tears welled in his eyes. When the string quartet finally appeared, Pericle wrapped up his song and let them take over.

Just as he was getting off the platform, he noticed a strikingly beautiful lady standing on the threshold, watching him intently.

Her hair was gathered in an elegant chignon and her blue dress was wrapped flatteringly around her figure. She was with a younger woman who looked a lot like her but lacked her quickness of eye and intensity of gaze. There was something odd about the pair, as if they didn't belong. Were they meant to be there? Were they lost?

As Don Pericle walked up to

them, he felt the older woman studying him just as he was studying her.

"My mother wants you to know that she greatly enjoyed your music." The younger woman spoke Italian with an English accent.

"Thank you," he said with a bow. He always found praise awkward, so he changed the subject. "Are you from the bride's or the groom's side?"

"Neither," the younger woman admitted. "We're looking for a venue for my wedding. Do you know if this villa is for hire?"

Don Pericle smiled. "Yes, it is."

The woman grinned and translated into English for her mother, who smiled too. "Can we speak to the person in charge of bookings?"

"Don Pericle is extremely busy at the moment, but you can meet him tomorrow at eleven," he told them.

***

Greta and Melanie drove back to their hotel in the old Sicilian village and asked the hotelier if he knew anything about the owner of the beautiful villa.

"Ah, the duke is a truly

remarkable man. His family used to own all the land from the seashore to the mountains, but they had squandered most of their fortune by the time it reached Don Pericle. Along with the ancestral home, he also inherited a mountain of debts," the man told them.

Greta's heart went out to the duke. When her husband died, he, too had left her a pile of debts.

"A lesser man would have sold Villa Lingualarga, but Don Pericle rolled up his sleeves and started the wedding business. He's not afraid of hard work. Sometimes his clients find him in the flowerbeds, up to his knees in soil, working late into the evening at an age when he should have long retired!"

Greta's heart squeezed. She should have retired long ago, too.

"Maybe he needs the money," she suggested.

"Yes, but he loves his job. Otherwise he would just organise the weddings."

"What else does he do?" Melanie asked.

"He counsels and advises. He's not afraid to cancel a wedding and lose money if he thinks that the couple should not be married. It's amazing how much he knows about love considering that he's been a bachelor all his life."

**

The next morning at eleven, mother and daughter were back at the villa. No music or tinkling of crockery filled the air this time, just birdsong. The pianist was waiting for them at the top of the staircase.

"Nice to see you again," he said, kissing their hands.

Greta couldn't remember the last time a man had kissed her hand.

"Hello. Is the duke available?" Melanie asked.

"That's me," the pianist said with a cheeky smile.

Greta's heart skipped a beat. The noble-hearted duke and the heart-rending pianist were one and the same!

He led them to a room clad in green damask which smelled of tobacco and leather. It was a true, old-fashioned man's study—elegant without pomposity, aged but not frayed, with earth tones and bursts of emerald, like the eyes of its owner sparkling against his olive skin.

They sat down and Melanie and the duke talked for a while in Italian, as Melanie explained how she and George had met and fallen in love in Sicily when they were students. It was then that Melanie had learned Italian.

Greta didn't understand much of what they were saying so she just enjoyed listening to the duke's voice, his vowels waxing and waning like the notes of his piano.

When he wrote *Melanie and George* on one of the pages of his diary, Greta's stomach flipped. Was it because they had secured a beautiful venue for the wedding reception, or because they now had a reason to see the duke again? Greta didn't know why that mattered, but it did.

***

The photoshoot went very well and it gave Greta enough money to buy a mother-of-the-bride outfit. It was only a week to the wedding and Greta was in her flat, trying to decide how she would carry her outfit on the aeroplane, when the phone rang.

"Mum, I have a problem."

Melanie's voice gave Greta a frisson of worry. "George and I are meant to meet with Don Pericle tomorrow, but we can't leave London due to work until the day before the wedding."

"Video conference him."

"Mum, he doesn't have a computer."

"Give him *carte blanche* on everything, then. You can trust his taste," Greta declared.

"I trust yours even more. It would put my mind at rest if you went to the meeting in our place."

The thought of being alone with

the duke unleashed a swarm of butterflies beneath Greta's breastbone. "OK. But warn him, will you? I don't want him to be disappointed to find out that I'm taking your place."

"I will. Thank you, Mum!"

Greta stuffed her wedding outfit into her suitcase and rang her travel agent to book the first flight to Sicily.

***

When Pericle saw a snow-white chignon emerge from the taxi's rear door, he felt his heart shift to a higher gear.

There was something about her that attracted and intrigued him. There was a depth to her eyes that talked to him. She was certainly a beautiful woman, and age seemed to suit her the way it suited a fine wine. It was such a shame that they didn't have a common language. Maybe French?

"Hello, Don Pericle," she said, offering her hand.

He kissed her hand. "Hello, Mrs Williams. Do you speak French?" he asked in the elegant French he had learnt at boarding school eons ago.

"*Oui,* yes, I do."

Excellent. "To what do I owe the pleasure of your visit?"

"Melanie and George are unable to leave London yet and have asked me to come in their place. I hope that you don't mind."

"It's a pleasure and an honour," he replied, offering his arm.

As soon as her hand rested gently on it, a tingle of pleasure ran up Pericle's arm and, to prolong that contact, he took her on a little tour of the villa.

She graciously approved his arrangements of draperies, flowers and party favours, which pleased him more than it should have. As she studied everything and made tasteful suggestions, Pericle studied her and found no possible suggestions for improvement.

Then he showed her the seating arrangement. "It is my understanding you'll be unaccompanied, but if I'm mistaken—"

"No, your seating plan is correct," Greta interrupted.

There was a meaningful pause, then they fell into conversation and opened up to each other with an ease that Pericle hadn't experienced before. She told him about her late husband, how he had left her destitute and how she was still modelling. The more they talked, the more Pericle felt that he had found somebody who could understand him. A twin soul.

At the end of her tour, she turned to him. "Thank you, Don Pericle. I am sure that Melanie will be very satisfied."

"Please, call me Pericle."

"And you can call me Greta. Thank you for your time. Would you be so kind as to call me a taxi back to my hotel?"

Pericle panicked. Was this the end of their time together? The next time he would see her, it would likely be at the wedding, together with lots of other people. An idea flashed across his mind. "Will you allow me to drive you?" he blurted out.

"That would be very pleasant."

Her smile encouraged him to be even more daring. "Or would you perhaps honour me with your presence for a little longer and be my guest? It can be lonely to stay in a hotel on your own."

She hesitated. Had he overstepped the line? He bowed. "I'm sorry for my impertinence, I should not have suggested—"

"I would be very glad to accept your hospitality."

***

So Greta spent the few days left until the wedding at Villa Lingualarga. She and Don Pericle strolled in the gardens, dined together, and chatted well into the night under the starry sky. It was bliss.

The words of the book of Genesis came to Pericle's mind: "It is not good for the man to be alone. I will make a helper suitable for him." For the first time since Laura's death, he felt that he had found company that suited him.

Laura. The thought made him shiver, though the night air was warm. Was he in danger of breaking the promise he had made to her that he would never love another woman again?

***

Villa Lingualarga reverberated with music, smelled of lemon blossoms and shone in the sunshine. Pericle couldn't have organised the wedding any better and the bride and the groom looked very happy.

Greta clapped and cheered and wished Melanie and George every happiness, but a lump of sadness was lodged in her throat. Was she sad because she would have no reason to see Pericle again after the wedding was over?

When the dancing started, she went looking for him. "Would it be untoward for a lady to invite a gentleman to dance?"

"It would only be a sign of the gentleman's slowness. Will you dance with me, Greta?"

"Yes, Pericle."

They locked hands and eyes and waltzed into the music.

"You should be very pleased with yourself. The party is going extremely well," she remarked.

"I am, but something else saddens me," he replied, looking deep into her eyes.

Like a mirror, his eyes reflected hers. "I believe it's a sadness we share."

Then Greta saw Pericle's eyes slip down to her lips and her heart skipped a beat. She shouldn't, but nothing could stop her yearning for his kiss.

"Greta, I—"

"Mum, come for a photo!" Melanie called from the edge of the dance floor.

"Sorry. I shouldn't be keeping the mother of the bride," Pericle said, and Greta's little bubble of hope shattered.

"My fault," she said airily, returning to her daughter's side.

***

Pericle sat at his desk with his accounts book open, but he couldn't concentrate. Although he hadn't felt like this for many years, he was confident in his diagnosis: he had fallen head over heels in love.

After that dance, he didn't manage to be alone with Greta again. Then she was gone, but not out of his heart.

The phone rang and jolted him out of his daydream.

"Hello! How is the duke of Lingualarga?" It was Antonio, Laura's brother.

When his fiancée had died, Pericle had grown very close to her brother, relishing their common memories of her. "Hello! How are you?"

"Not too well, actually. Recovering from surgery, so I won't be able to visit the crypt with you this year."

Every year on the anniversary of Laura's death, Pericle visited her family's home, a couple of hours' drive away, and he would go to the family crypt with her brother. Was it only a coincidence that, just when Pericle was in danger of breaking his promise, Antonio refused to accompany him to Laura's tomb?

Pericle didn't answer, so Antonio continued. "I'd come with you but, unless you carry me down the stairs of the crypt on your back, I can't."

That image was enough to steal a laugh from Pericle.

"This old bull might carry you down, but I wouldn't trust him to pull you back up again," he joked.

When he put down the phone, Pericle sank into his chair. Was Antonio's call a heavenly reminder that, by allowing himself to think about Greta, he was taking a grave risk with his own heart and with the sacred memory of Laura?

What madness had got into him to make him break his word at seventy-six, when he had lasted his entire life without a woman?

***

Later in the week, Pericle was packing for his trip when the phone rang again. He picked up, and his heart stopped at the sound of a voice he remembered very well. Greta. Maybe forgetting her wasn't going to be as simple as he had hoped.

"Hello, Greta. How are you?"

"I have good news." She

hesitated. "I've shown fashion editors photos of the wedding and they're very impressed. They would love to do a photoshoot in Villa Lingualarga, and they asked me to model."

Pericle was left speechless. Joy and fear cavorted in his heart. There was nothing he wished more than to see Greta again, but wouldn't that make it more difficult to keep his promise?

"If you don't want to open your home to the public, I understand. I'm sorry to have asked."

"I'm more than happy to host the

photoshoot. When?"

"Next month. The fifteenth."

His blood ran cold. That was the anniversary of Laura's death. That coincidence couldn't be down to chance—he was being asked to choose between Laura and Greta.

Throughout his life he had always chosen the most honourable path and this time would be no exception. He would leave his second-in-command to meet Greta and the photographers.

"That date is fine," he told Greta.

***

On seeing Antonio, it was clear

to Pericle that he did not have long left on this earth.

He felt a pang of sadness. Antonio wasn't just his best friend and almost a brother, but he was also the only person with whom he could talk about Laura. Antonio had been by Laura's bed when she was slipping away, when Pericle had spoken the fateful words that had bound him for life.

Pericle took his pipe out of his mouth and dropped his head.

"Don't be sad," Antonio said, letting out a little puff of smoke. "If it's nice on the other side, I will rush back and take you with me! Mind you, you're still strong. Have you decided when you're finally going to become frail?"

"As long as there are couples that want to get married in Villa Lingualarga, I'm not allowed to." Pericle smiled.

"That must be the secret! How could it have taken me so long to work it out?"

"Work out what?"

"That the secret to your health is that you help others get married, but you never marry yourself. It's marriage and family that wear a man down. But you are like Cupid."

"The story goes that Cupid eventually falls in love, too, but it's all rather difficult for him," Pericle corrected him, then a shadow fell over his heart. "You know very well why I have never married."

Antonio raised his eyebrows. "But you were only twenty-one when it all happened."

"A promise is a promise."

"Goodness, I didn't think..." Antonio looked shocked. "I mean, nobody would hold you accountable for anything said in such circumstances! My parents would always ask me if you had found love again. They were very anxious that you should find happiness after everything you'd lost. I feel sorry for you, Pericle. We should have had this conversation much earlier. I hope that you haven't closed the door of your heart because of this promise."

Pericle squeezed his arm. "Don't worry. I had never met a woman who made it difficult to keep the promise..."

They both took a sip from their coffee cups.

"...until now," he continued. "But I fear I've lost her already. She's in Villa Lingualarga right now and I haven't even welcomed her."

"Goodness me! Go home, get your girl back and let me know that you have so I can die happy."

Pericle hugged his friend one last time and set off in a desperate hurry. Nevertheless, on the way, he stopped at the crypt. He laid a bunch of lilies on Laura's sandstone sarcophagus and stroked the cheeks of the statue carved on the lid.

As a ray of sun entered through

a slit high up in the wall and caressed her lips, the statue seemed to smile. Pericle looked up to the light and tears welled in his eyes. Heaven had freed him from a promise to which he had stubbornly bound himself for years. Heaven would ensure that he wasn't too late for Greta.

He kissed the statue's stone cheeks and drove home as fast as he could.

***

Greta leaned on the parapet of Villa Lingualarga's balcony, fixing her eyes on the horizon like

Penelope waiting for Ulysses.

"Good job, everyone," the photographer called.

The crew started loading the equipment into their vans, but Greta didn't move.

She should have known better than to fall in love again. Men had loved her and left her too many times. She had thought that with Pericle it would be different, but he hadn't even been there to meet her. She had organised the photoshoot just to be with him once again, and he had run away.

She should be getting out of her

flowing silk dress and removing the rose from her hair, but she didn't feel like it. She didn't feel like doing anything.

Then the music of a mandolin reached her ears. It was tentative at first, then more confident, rising up from the garden below.

She couldn't help imagining that the man she loved was serenading her from under the balcony. The vision became more vivid when a voice joined the music and the melody turned into a song that talked about love, regrets and forgiveness.

Goosebumps covered her skin as her heart told her that it was Pericle. She lowered her gaze. He was there, on one knee, serenading her on his mandolin. Her heart felt like a bird soaring up into the sky.

She took the rose out of her hair, kissed it, and let it float down to him.

***

Greta finally told Melanie the truth about everything: her financial situation and her work, plus her affection for Pericle and his subsequent proposal, which she had accepted.

Much to Greta's relief, Melanie wholeheartedly approved of him. "So long as you don't expect me to call you Duchess, Mum."

Villa Lingualarga was prepared for yet another wedding, but this time it was the owner's. Pericle and Greta didn't want any fuss to be made of them, but the whole village turned up with gifts for them.

Pericle's sisters, nephews and nieces were thrilled, and many of Greta's friends attended, too. Melanie and George glowed, as enamoured with each other as at their own wedding.

Even Antonio was there, having decided not to leave this world before seeing his best friend's own happy ending.

4. TAKING THE TEST

"I want to drive. I want to try the driving test," Melina told him.

"Again?" Tanino said, putting down the crossword.

"I'm older and wiser now."

Tanino wasn't too sure about the

wiser part. "It isn't about age or wisdom, Melina. You couldn't stand all the other cars and the scooters zooming around you. Palermo's traffic hasn't got any better."

"I won't fail my test this time. I want to drive."

"Why? I always take you anywhere you want."

"Last week I asked you to drive me to church and you didn't."

"The football was on! Anyway, you could have walked: it was only drizzling and you're not made of sugar."

"Are you saying that I'm bitter?"

"It's just a figure of speech. I could just as well have said salt."

"But you chose sugar."

Tanino ran a hand over his face. Oh, how he wished he had missed the football and driven her to church! Melina behind the wheel was the last thing he needed. Trying to teach her to drive had taken years off his life, not to mention all the sleep he lost, due to worry, every afternoon when she went out in the driving instructor's car.

"Apart from last week, when have I ever refused to drive you somewhere?"

"That time I wanted to go to my sister."

"The car had broken down."

"I want to be free to go wherever I want."

"Where do you want to go?"

"*Where* is not the point. The point is that I won't have to ask you," she said, and disappeared in the kitchen.

Tanino imagined returning home for lunch one day and finding his wife missing—gone on a road trip from Sicily to the Alps. Even the thought was too much to bear.

He sighed, picked up the remote controller and turned on the TV. Thankfully, the football was on.

***

After the six o'clock Mass, Melina shared her problem with her friends.

"He doesn't want you to go gallivanting about without him," Peppina said.

"This is about power, that's what it is," Anna said.

"It's very simple: he doesn't think that Melina can do it," Rosaria said, "and he worries that she'll scratch the car."

"Whatever the reason, Tanino is against it, and Melina must get her driving licence," Peppina declared, and everyone nodded.

After supper, instead of washing up, Melina went down to the garage and sat in the car.

It had been such a long time since her last attempt that she had forgotten where everything was. She turned on the lights, swished the wipers and flicked the indicator, but that was not what she was looking for.

When she finally found the horn, she gave three ceremonial blasts to seal her resolution.

***

Melina hadn't mentioned her desire to drive to Tanino again so he was convinced that she had gone off the idea.

One evening, he was trying to cross the road when a car stopped to let him through. It was a rare kindness in Palermo's evening rush hour so he raised his hand in thanks and started crossing.

But a blast of that car's horn made him jump out of his skin. He scowled at the driver through the windscreen and froze. The driver was Melina! Yes, she was behind the wheel of a driving instructor's car, but was it safe? Was the instructor paying attention? Was he qualified? He looked very young.

Tanino felt instantly dizzy. Some of the cars behind Melina started honking. Oh, how Tanino hated it when other motorists hooted at his wife! What if they made her panic and she lost control? Tanino felt the need to steady himself, so he leaned against the bonnet.

The driving instructor leapt out of the car. "You're alright, aren't you? We didn't touch you!"

What was he doing, leaving Melina alone in the car? Tanino wanted to shout at him to get back into the vehicle, but all that came out of his throat were little gasps.

Meanwhile other motorists had gathered around them.

"What's going on?"

"A pedestrian's been hit."

"Call the ambulance!"

Melina stuck her head out the window. "Get into the car, Tanino, and stop making a fuss. I never would have thought that you would stoop this low! Faking an accident just to stop me getting a licence!"

The little crowd of other motorists booed and scowled at him. For the first time in his life, Tanino was quick to clamber into a car driven by his wife. Paradoxically, he felt safer inside than out.

Melina drove much better than he remembered, but Tanino noticed that the instructor wasn't giving her any advice.

Once she had completed a difficult piece of parallel parking in front of the driving school, the young man scribbled something on his clipboard. Then he turned to her and smiled.

"Congratulations, you've passed your test."

Tanino almost fainted.

When they reached their flat, it was past eight o'clock. Tanino was flooded with weariness. "What are we going to do about supper?"

Melina smiled. "You lay the table while I go and get some take-away roast chicken." With that, she whipped the car keys out of the cabinet and left.

Tanino went to bed. He was no longer hungry.

***

"That was my parking space!" Melina shouted. She blasted the horn for good measure.

Tanino regretted asking Melina to drive him to his eye appointment at the hospital. "Just drop me off here and meet me inside once you've found another parking space."

But all through the eye examination Tanino could not stop worrying.

"You can relax, I'm not going to hurt you," the doctor told him.

"I'm worried about my wife getting hurt, not me," Tanino replied.

The man gave him a strange look and checked his reflexes one more time.

But Melina still hadn't turned up.

"At least if she has an accident she'll be near the hospital," he said, trying to reassure himself.

When he was finally released, Tanino rushed outside and there she was! She had stopped in the ambulance queue and was arguing with the hospital's staff.

***

The news of Melina's successful driving test spread, and the next time it rained around the time of

Mass, everyone expected to see her arrive at the wheel of her car.

Instead, it was Tanino who drove up to the church, stopped in front of the entrance and offered her an umbrella.

"Melina, why haven't you driven yourself?" Peppina asked.

Melina flapped an airy hand. "I can't be bothered with the hassle of parking. Having a driver is much better."

"Doesn't Tanino mind?" Anna asked.

"It seems not." Melina shrugged. "Don't ask me why, but he says that driving me about is much better for his health."

5. STARS ARE SILVER

Giovanni turned off the TV and sighed. Back in the day, there wasn't an afternoon when he didn't stumble across one of his films when flicking channels, and he couldn't go to the shops without passers-by asking for an autograph.

But these days his films weren't being aired much. Lots of new movies, soaps, and TV series had been shot since he had last been in Cinecittà, Rome's movie-set city.

Someone once asked the unrivalled film director Federico Fellini which city he would like to live in, and he replied without hesitation, "Cinecittà". Giovanni would have said the same.

He stepped out onto the terrace of his rooftop flat and admired the vast expanse of Rome, and Cinecittà in the distance. The city that made dreams come true.

It was there that he had met Antonietta, and there that they'd parted.

"Work and love don't marry," she told him that day.

"But we are married," he replied.

"That was the mistake."

When they had finished starring in the same series and started working on different projects, their gruelling and conflicting shooting schedules had pulled them apart. They had sacrificed love on the altar of career.

The phone rang and he padded

back inside. "Hello?"

"How are you, old sport?"

Only his agent talked to him like that, but it couldn't be him. Giovanni was the one who called first these days, usually to find out if there was any work for him. "Who's calling?"

"Now you don't recognise your beloved agent?"

Giovanni's hands turned clammy. This call was either very good news or very bad—most likely the latter. Maybe someone had used the shampoo from his latest TV commercial and had had his scalp burned? "Hi, Pippo. How are you? Is everything OK?"

"More than OK! You'd better sit down, mate."

With his heart in his mouth, Giovanni plonked himself on to the sofa. "Tell me."

"Francesca Antico is thinking of casting you for her new TV medical drama. It's going to be big."

For a piece of news like this, sitting down wasn't enough. Giovanni plonked down onto the cushions. Why was there so little air in the room?

His agent continued. "I bet you

thought that you were going to spend the rest of your life pottering around your flat. If that's the case, you can change your plans immediately. And start taking vitamins, too, because you're not allowed to give up the ghost for the foreseeable future: you're my goose that lays golden eggs."

Trust Pippo to think about money. "How much are they offering?" Giovanni managed to croak through the knot in his throat.

"They haven't said yet, because, unfortunately, there is a condition to you getting the job. Francesca grew up watching 'Dottori Innamorati'..."

That was the TV series where he'd met Antonietta and their love blossomed. Whenever they had to kiss for the camera, they kissed for real. At the end of the series, they got married.

"... and she wants to cast both of you. If she can't have you both, she'll have neither."

Now Giovanni needed more than a little lie-down on the sofa. He needed a strong whisky.

"What's your situation with

Antonietta? Are you still in touch?" Pippo asked.

"We haven't spoken since the divorce."

"I see... I don't want to pry into your personal life, but in this case your personal life and your work are woven together. At the time when you split up, the tabloids said that it was a consensual parting, but I never believe a word they say. Tell me the truth: has Antonietta any reasons to hold a grudge?"

"Whether she harbours any resentment against me, I don't

know. But if you're asking whether I cheated on her, the answer is absolutely not. I don't think she blames me for our break-up. It was the pressure of work that pulled us apart."

"Good. Still, you'd better open a tab with the florist, just in case. Good luck. Let me know as soon as you've spoken to her."

"*Me* speak to her? No, no, no. This is an agent's job. It's your job to contact her agent and her agent's job to inform her."

"I'm sure that Francesca Antico has already contacted Antonietta's agent. I'm not saying that you should break the news to her. All I'm saying is that you should talk to her and iron out any reservations. If she holds any grudges against you and doesn't want to take on the job, you sort them out."

"Why aren't you asking me if I hold any grudges or have reservations about working with her?" Giovanni asked.

"Because you can't refuse this job, or you'll have to deal with yours truly."

***

Antonietta had just emerged from a long, luxurious bath when the house phone rang.

Nobody called her on her landline these days. She was tempted to ignore it, but as her mobile had been out of charge all day, virtually cutting her off from the world, she didn't mind speaking to any human being, even if just to tell them that she was happy with her current phone contract.

"Hello?"

There was silence at the other end. "Antonietta?"

Her heart somersaulted in her

chest. It was Giovanni's voice. It couldn't be him. She didn't even know if he was still alive. She had never given in to the temptation to look him up on Facebook or the internet. "Who's calling?" she answered warily.

"Giovanni."

Oh, heavens. She grabbed the door jamb to steady herself. A chair. She needed a chair, or it'd be the floor soon. She stumbled to the bed and dropped on to it.

"Antonietta...are you still there?"

That voice. It hadn't changed. He sounded just like the last time she'd spoken to him, thirty years ago. His handsome face flashed across her mind, and a lot of other memories that weren't very helpful at that moment.

"Yes," she said in a strangled voice.

"How are you?" He sounded tentative and shy.

"Fine."

A beat of silence at the other end. Maybe her one-word answer had come across as cold and unfriendly, but there was so much to tell each other after so many years that she didn't know where to start. And one word was all she could manage to heave out of her constricted chest.

"I'm sorry to disturb you. I guess that you've heard already that our paths are crossing again...but they don't have to, if you don't want. I don't mean that I don't—far from it—but just that I don't want to presume that you do... Oh, what a muddle! Sorry. Please, say something."

"I don't know what you're talking about."

"You don't know?"

"I have no idea."

Of course, luck would have it that, of all the days, something important should happen when her mobile was out of action.

"Francesca Antico is shooting a new medical drama and, being a fan of our 'Dottori Innamorati', she wants to cast us. I'm not sure what our roles would be, but I know that there's a condition: we must both accept the parts. Francesca will have both of us or neither."

"I see."

There was so much she wanted to ask him—how has your life been? Are you well? Have you got someone else?—but she didn't trust her voice not to betray the emotions running riot in her chest. And this was clearly a business call.

"I'm sorry, I've clearly disturbed you at a bad time. You can think about what you want to do and let me know through your agent. I won't keep you any long—"

"I accept."

***

Crossing the gates of Cinecittà, Giovanni felt like he was home again. He belonged here.

But the joy of the return was marbled with anxiety. Was he

going to be up to the job? In the last few years, he had shot nothing but TV commercials.

Most of all, he was apprehensive about meeting Antonietta. When he entered the studio, his heart thumped even before seeing her. They had always had a special awareness of each other.

"Hello everyone," he said jovially.

Francesca Antico came forward and shook his hand energetically, telling him how big a fan of his she was, but all Giovanni could think of was Antonietta.

As soon as he lifted his gaze to

her, she smiled at him, causing considerable turbulence in his heart.

"Now, let me tell you a bit about this project. This is a medical drama with a strong romantic element. Your characters are madly in love but are afraid of embarking on a workplace romance that could hurt their careers."

Giovanni swallowed. So this was a romantic part. He had assumed that, at their age, they wouldn't be given such roles in the story. Those were for the young and beautiful. Not that Antonietta wasn't still beautiful—quite the opposite, actually.

"Any questions?" the director asked.

"Yes," Antonietta said. "Who are the leading characters in this series?"

Francesca smiled. "You."

Crikey. They had the leading roles! Antonietta's slightly parted lips told him that she was as surprised as he was.

"You'll be remunerated accordingly, of course, but that's something to discuss with your agents once we decide that we can work together. If you don't have any more questions, we can move on and try out one of the scenes. Here is the script. I want scene eight, please," she said, handing them a wad of paper each.

They sat down and read. It was a love scene. A little voice in Giovanni's head told him to stand up and run away at once.

Cradling Antonietta in his arms, kissing her, listening to her saying that she loved him, was playing with fire. He couldn't afford to put his heart on the line like that.

But then another voice in his

head reminded him that he wasn't the only person concerned: if he pulled out, Antonietta wouldn't get the job, their agents would miss out on their fat commissions, and Francesca wouldn't see her favourite childhood actors back on stage. Pulling out from this project would be the most selfish thing he could do.

He took a deep breath and tried to memorise the lines. Thank goodness that he had slapped on some extra aftershave before leaving the house.

***

Antonietta felt her cheeks warm up as she read the script. No, she couldn't do this. Not with Giovanni.

It had taken her years to get over him, and finding herself in his arms while he kissed her and whispered that he loved her risked undoing all her hard work. Surely he was going to refuse the part.

She glanced at him, imagining that any moment he'd throw the script to the floor and storm off with a horrified face. Instead, he had his reading glasses firmly on his nose and was poring over the pages as if his eyes were the laser beam of a photocopier. If she pulled out of this, he wouldn't get the part, and she couldn't do that to him.

He had never done anything to deserve this. They had broken up because, when they'd had to choose between career and love, they had chosen their careers. Maybe he would have chosen love if she had given him the chance. She had happily trampled over her own heart before, and it would be hypocritical to choose heart over career now. She pushed her reading glasses up her nose and continued reading.

As soon as Francesca sat down in the director's chair, Antonietta closed her eyes and imagined that she was Giorgia the surgeon. The lights went on and the cameras rolled.

"I don't know what to do," she said.

"The patient's notes say that the appendix has to come out," Giovanni said.

"Move closer to each other," Francesca bellowed.

They stepped closer and she smelled Giovanni's aftershave.

Memories flooded back and rocked her before she pushed them away.

Where was she? A quick glance at the script saved her. "I don't mean about the patient. I mean about us."

Giovanni's chest heaved and brushed against her arm, unravelling her a little more.

"There's only one thing to do about us, Antonietta."

Antonietta? Her character was called Giorgia.

He held her arms, turned her around and kissed her. It was a real kiss, no pretence, just like in the old times.

Her kneecaps instantly melted. Thank goodness he was holding her arms.

"Excellent!" Francesca shouted. "You've got the parts. I knew that you two would be fantastic together, but I had no idea that you could even make yourselves blush on command!"

***

How could he have made a mistake like that—saying her name instead of her character's? It had never happened before. It must be his old brain. Or maybe it was a

Freudian slip.

And then the kiss. He had crossed the line. He had completely forgotten that he was acting. He had better apologise to Antonietta, or at least talk to her.

At the end of the session, he hung back to catch her.

"Are you free for a bite of lunch?"

What had come out of his mouth wasn't what he had intended to say. He should have just apologised then and there.

"I'm sorry, I'm... busy. See you next week," she said, avoiding his gaze.

"Sure, I'm sorry..."

But she was gone.

***

Antonietta got home and immediately ran a bath with mountains of bubbles. Bubble baths were her coping method when she was troubled or down. She should be celebrating—her agent surely was—but instead all she could think of was Giovanni's loving gaze and burning kiss.

No, she shouldn't be so silly as to get ideas. He was an actor, and a very fine one, too. He had only done his job.

But why would he let her name slip? Did he still have feelings for her? Surely not.

The following week, she was back at the studio with trepidation. She had studied the script and there were no kisses in the episode. The two characters would just be working together in the hospital. But just the thought of seeing Giovanni again rocked her a little.

She walked into the studio holding the script against her chest like a shield. As usual, she sensed his presence in the room even before she saw him. She avoided looking in his direction and sensed that he was doing the same.

She got herself into professional mode and was pleased with her performance. At the end, Francesca congratulated them. "It was excellent. You really managed to show that awkwardness between two people in love who are desperately trying to hide their feelings."

Antonietta smiled wryly. Maybe the scene had come out well because she hadn't needed to act.

Yes, she still had feelings for Giovanni—the only man she had ever loved, married and, inexplicably, divorced.

"As we've finished early with this scene, I'd like to do another. Episode seven, scene five, needs the same set. I'll give you some time to study the script."

Oh, no. A love scene.

***

"No, no, no!" Francesca called out, springing up from her chair. "It's not time to be awkward around each other anymore. We are much further into the series now. Let the passion show."

Giovanni ran a hand over his face. He couldn't do another kiss like the one in the first rehearsal. That kiss hadn't been just work and Antonietta had made it clear that their relationship should be just that. It wouldn't be fair on her. Certainly not without discussing things with her.

"Can we take a break and start again after lunch?" Antonietta suggested.

"Fine. See you at two."

On the way out of the room, Antonietta walked up to him. "Is your invitation to lunch still open?"

"Sure." It was time they had a frank conversation.

The café in Cinecittà had a nice outside seating area.

"Isn't it good that we can now sit out without fear of paparazzi?" he said, biting into a pizzetta.

"If this series takes off, our freedom might not last. We'd better enjoy it."

She stretched out her arms and closed her eyes in the sun. Her silver hair glittered in the sunshine. She was so beautiful.

He let his gaze linger on her a

little too long and, when she opened her eyes again, she caught him looking at her.

"I'm sorry about the kiss the other day—"

"Francesca liked it."

"But you didn't?"

"I did." She blushed.

Giovanni's heart cavorted in his chest. He stretched his hand across the table. "I don't think I've ever stopped loving you, Antonietta."

She smiled. "I don't think I did, either. Do you remember when I said that work and love don't marry?" she said.

"How could I forget?"

"I was wrong. I was determined to shine like the sun and any obstacle that could slow down my ascent, I'd incinerate out of my way. Including love. But now I've learned that the sun is lonely. It's much better to be one of the stars. They have each other's company. Is it too late for us, Giovanni?"

He stroked her hand. "No. Love is made to last forever. The sun is golden, but the stars are silver, just like us."

They leaned across the table and kissed.

6. THE GREATEST GIFT

"Tanino, do you know that Giovanna got a ruby from Luigi for their ruby anniversary?" Melina said when she got back from church.

Oh, no. The 29th of this month would mark their 55th wedding anniversary.

Tanino wondered what expensive stone a 55th wedding anniversary would be named after, but he didn't need to ask—Melina volunteered the information.

"Fifty-five years is an emerald anniversary. Emerald symbolises eternity and commitment."

Was that because sticking together for fifty-five years felt like an eternity? Tanino thought better of saying this.

It wasn't that he didn't love Melina. On the contrary, he would give not one but both his kidneys for her, and lungs, too (the heart, he had already given her).

But he didn't believe in soppy romanticism. For him, love was cooking the other person's favourite meal—the Sicilian pasta with sardines and fennel was his. Changing the lightbulb of her bedside lamp so that she could read in bed. Helping look for a misplaced pair of reading glasses.

"Who decided on emeralds? The jewellers?" he grumbled.

"You're not funny."

"I'm not joking. It was a diamond mining company that started the fashion of diamond engagement rings, did you know?"

"Well, the next big anniversary after emerald is diamond." Melina thrust a magazine under his gaze. On a page, all the wedding anniversaries were laid out on a table and matched with a mishmash of materials that ranged from cotton to platinum.

Tanino shook his head. "It makes no sense: when a man is young and still in employment, the anniversaries are cheap stuff like cotton, paper and leather. But when the poor fellow is retired, he has to dish out rubies, emeralds and diamonds. If you ask me, this is all completely topsy-turvy."

"It's not. The longer the people have been together, the bigger the prize," Melina said smugly.

"Because marriage is an endurance race, of course," he teased.

She snorted and strode off to the kitchen.

Tanino trudged to the balcony to tend his roses, wondering if there would be any dinner for him that night.

***

Why couldn't Tanino be a little more romantic? Men were such cheats: they gave you flowers, sang love songs and murmured sweet nonsense into your ears when they were courting you, only to stop once they'd secured you in marriage.

They turned from Cupid, the Roman god of love, to Mars, the god of war—that was when, heaven forbid, they didn't turn into Bacchus, the god of wine!

Melina let out a sigh and her nostrils filled with a smell of burning. Oh, no, she had burned the dinner!

Oh, well, Tanino didn't like lentils anyway, and she didn't mind if they were a little 'roasted'. Tanino would complain, though. He had become very fussy about food. Her mamma had warned her: as they grow old, men think of nothing but what they're having for their next meal.

Melina shook off her reverie and drained the pasta, which had irreparably turned to gloop.

***

When Tanino sank his fork into the white and brown goo he could hardly tell that it was pasta with lentils. His least favourite food, and now it was cooked to death, too.

But he refrained from any comment. This was clearly his punishment for teasing Melina about wedding anniversary gifts.

"What happened to the mandolin that you used to serenade me with when you were young? Have you still got it?"

Tanino frowned. Where was this conversation going? "No. Our daughter rode her tricycle over it."

"Ah, yes." Melina's face lit up. "We should buy you another one."

"Wouldn't the money be better spent on a new shopping trolley? One of the wheels looked wobbly when you came back from the market yesterday."

"The wheel is the least of its problems: the handle came off while I was crossing the road."

Tanino's heart squeezed as he imagined Melina struggling with a runaway trolley in the midst of zooming cars.

"But I've repaired it," she added, lifting her chin.

This was even more worrying. The last time Melina had 'repaired' something, she had used sticky tape and jute string on a kitchen pot's handle.

"Pity about the mandolin," she said with a slightly theatrical sigh.

Tanino felt defensive. Was she accusing him of deliberately not replacing the broken mandolin?

"It's lucky at least that I have dried and kept the flowers you gave me on our first date." She tutted.

Tanino felt at a loss about Melina's logic. What was the connection between the broken mandolin and the dried flowers?

Were they talking about the durability of objects? About preserving stuff from the past? "There are some nice things from my mother's flat in the garage, if you want to take a look."

Melina shot him a narrowed-eyed look.

"There's none more deaf than the one who doesn't want to hear," she hissed, then got up to clear the table.

Tanino, puzzled but relieved that that the meal was over, got up and went to the store cupboard to check on Melina's trolley.

***

Melina didn't sleep well. How could Tanino be so insensitive?

He didn't care about her anymore. He only cared about his plants, which he watered and checked every night for parasites. He collected rain just to water them, and squashed any aphids he found between his forefinger and thumb with infinite patience.

The next morning, Melina picked up her shopping list and her handbag, then went to the store cupboard to get her trolley.

The wool that she had used to

tie the handle had disappeared. Melina gave it a little tug and found that the handle didn't come off. Tanino must have done something to it. Was he trying to say that her repair wasn't good enough?

At the market, Pippo the fishmonger saw her coming. "Signora Melina, my swordfish is so fresh that the sardines in its stomach are still swimming!" he sang to her in his operatic baritone.

"Then I shall have the sardines, because they'll cost me less," she answered.

It was part of their normal banter preceding a sale. In the end, she would usually buy what he recommended, but only after making him shave something off the price.

"Swordfish is your husband's favourite," he retorted.

"Today isn't his birthday. He can eat sardines."

But Pippo had cut two generous slices of swordfish and wrapped them in waterproof paper. "I'll give you a good price, my lady. How much do you want to pay for these?"

"Five euros."

"Eight."

"Seven."

"Seven fifty."

A beat of silence and the price was agreed.

Just as Melina opened her wallet to pay, a hand landed on her shoulder.

"Melina, my dear, how are you?"

It was Giovanna. Immediately, Melina's eyes swivelled to her friend's left hand, where an eternity ring studded with rubies and diamonds winked coquettishly at her. Melina felt a cold and spiky lump of envy, hard and green as an emerald, embed in her chest.

"Your swordfish is ready, my beautiful lady," Pippo's gravelly voice boomed.

He had called her 'beautiful'. When was the last time Tanino had paid her any compliment?

The fishmonger smiled jovially, Giovanna's ring twinkled in the sunlight, and Melina's resentment boiled like ruby-red hot lava.

"I've changed my mind. I want sardines," she said.

Pippo rolled his eyes and, holding a hand to his chest, groaned as if he had been hit in the heart by an arrow. "My heart aches, but your wish is my command."

Back home, the fennel fronds endured a vicious chopping, the soaked sultana were squeezed almost dry in Melina's fists, and the sardines' backbones were shot into the bin like arrows as Melina took out on them her frustration against her wicked husband.

***

Tanino found himself standing in front of the jeweller's window without knowing how or why he had got there.

He had left the house to buy a new plant for the balcony but found himself walking past the jeweller's. The window glittered and twinkled like a galaxy. It was a sight to behold but, as in every galaxy, there were black holes—the plastic tags with the prices: 599 euros, 1,999 euros.

The only things that were remotely affordable were simple chains and plain silver or gold bands. Well, there was no way he was going to spend hundreds of euros on a green stone and some yellow metal. He swivelled on his heels and walked on to the plant shop where he bought a luxuriant potted rose, then went back home.

When the lift doors opened on to his floor the unmistakable scent of sardines and wild fennel filled his lungs.

Could he be so lucky that the smell was coming from his flat? There were two apartments on his floor and the chances that Melina would be cooking his favourite dish today, of all days, were near zero.

Yet when he opened the door of his flat, the smell of wild fennel and fish meandered through the red rose plant in his arms and dived straight into his nostrils.

"I'm ho-ome!" he called from door.

This was the signal for Melina to drop the pasta in the boiling water. She would only do it when he got home because, once the pasta was in, dinner could not be delayed.

Without changing into his slippers or even putting the heavy plant down, he scuttled into the kitchen. There was his Melina, bent over the bubbling pot, energetically stirring the pasta. For him.

Tanino's heart filled with song.

"My darling, oh, how I love you when you cook for me!" he cried.

Melina whipped her head round. As her surprised gaze slipped from his face to the roses he was holding, a smile curled her lips and her eyes lit up.

With rare quickness of thought he thrust the blooming pot towards her. "For you!"

Melina dropped her wooden spoon and her smile reached the wrinkles on the sides of her eyes. "Oh, Tanino! You shouldn't have!" she said, taking the plant from him.

Then he hugged her and kissed her like he hadn't done in a while.

***

On their anniversary Melina felt contented. Looking at it from a practical angle, a plant was better than a bunch of flowers because it would continue to flower year after year—especially if it came with the warranty that Tanino would be looking after it lovingly for her.

As they sat at the table eating *pasta con le sarde* again and drinking wine, she admired her rose on the balcony. It now had more flowers than on the day she had received it. Then, she had a jolt.

"Tanino, I've only just noticed! The flowers are red like rubies, and the leaves are green like emeralds. Oh, aren't you a hopeless romantic!"

7. STOP THE WEDDING!

Panic seized Giulia when the car stopped outside Villa Lingualarga. *It's normal to be nervous at your wedding*, she reminded herself.

But something inside her clamoured that this was more than normal bride's nerves. It felt more like the last desperate cry of a wild animal about to be caged. A shaft of sunlight lit up the villa's grand façade, dazzling her almost as much as the feeling that she didn't want this wedding. In front of her, at the top of the wide baroque staircase, stood Riccardo in his three-piece suit.

How had she got herself into this situation? He hadn't even proposed to her. His mother had taken them aside one day after a family lunch and told them sternly that it was high time they got married. So the wedding had been organised.

Run away, a voice in her head shouted. But all her family and friends were lining the staircase, ready to throw confetti and cheer for the happy couple. It was too late.

***

Valeria hadn't liked the look on her daughter's face at breakfast that morning. It was the look of a wild animal startled by a car headlight.

She had put it down to wedding stress, like she had done with all the other oddities of the last few months.

But now, as Giulia emerged from the bridal car, Valeria saw that look again. Her daughter's smile was tight and brittle, her eyes wide and scared, and suddenly Valeria was sure, as only a mother can be, that Giulia was not happy about marrying Riccardo.

As remorse squeezed her heart, adrenaline flooded her mind. She must stop the wedding. Should she step out on to the bride's path and block her way up? Should she shout out?

What if she were wrong? She would have needlessly ruined her daughter's wedding day.

Valeria tried to catch her husband's eye, but he was concentrating on his job of delivering their daughter to her fiancé at the top of the stairs. She must find a way to pause the wedding and speak to Giulia in private.

Valeria rushed to the wedding organiser and host, who stood at the bottom of the stairs, surveying and smiling.

"Don Pericle, I must speak to my daughter now. I need you to pause the ceremony," she panted.

The duke's relaxed smile turned into bewilderment. "Pause the wedding?"

Giulia and Tommaso were already halfway up the staircase.

"I fear that Giulia is not sure about this marriage."

***

It took a couple of seconds for Don Pericle to register what the mother of the bride was telling him. When it sank in, it shook him like a gale.

Before agreeing to host a wedding, he always interviewed the couple to make sure that they were willing, suited and ready to get married.

He had always taken great pride in his intuition, but if Signora Alcamo's hunch was correct, on this occasion he had failed. Most importantly, he now had to put things right.

Interpreting his silence as reluctance, the mother-of-the-bride pressed on. "I don't need long. Just a few seconds to talk to my daughter,"

"Of course," he replied reassuringly, but when he looked up the stairs and saw the bride switching from her father's arm to her fiancé's, his confidence faltered.

It wouldn't be long before Giulia and Riccardo would be standing in front of the mayor, saying their vows.

He sneaked away to the back of the garden, where a secret hatch led underground. He lifted it and descended some damp, slippery steps.

Guided only by touch and memory, he followed a narrow tunnel to a spiral staircase. Thick cobwebs tickled his nose and the strong musty smell tickled his throat. He climbed as fast as the stale air of the narrow space allowed. He hoped that the door at the other end would open after all these years of disuse.

Giulia and Riccardo must have reached the end of the corridor by now. He had to hurry, but the spiral staircase was making him dizzy.

He met the door so unexpectedly and with such momentum that the impact made it burst open.

A shriek told him that he had sprung out of the wall quite close to the couple. The sudden light and fresh air revived him, and he glided to the far end of the ballroom, where the mayor was behind a desk draped in velvet and tassels.

The guests, who had been staring at the door to catch the couple's entry, murmured in surprise when he appeared instead, all sprinkled with dust and wrapped in cobwebs.

"*Signor Sindaco*, we must pause the ceremony," he panted to the mayor.

The man's eyes bulged. "Why don't you take a seat and have

some water?"

"I am serious, Sindaco. There might be an impediment to this marriage."

The mayor was not an unreasonable man, but he was a stickler for protocol. "If there is an impediment, let those who have shared it with you speak out at the appointed time during the ceremony."

He looked away from Don Pericle and smiled at the incoming couple, making clear that he wasn't going to let an eccentric old aristocrat waste any more of anyone's time.

Meanwhile, the bride and groom had almost reached the desk. The expression on the bride's face deeply troubled Don Pericle. She looked like a woman hoping that something—anything—would stop her wedding.

So Don Pericle took the matter into his own hands. "I am sorry, but we have to pause the ceremony!" he declared loudly.

The violins stopped and a stunned silence crashed into the room like an uninvited guest.

The fog that had shrouded the bride's face like a grey veil gave way to a hopeful, tentative smile. It was enough to reassure Don Pericle that he was doing the right thing.

"What are you doing, Don Pericle?" the mayor protested.

Pericle ignored him. "This villa is haunted..."

Some of the guests sneered, a few arched their eyebrows, while others looked nervously behind. The bride continued to smile.

"... and its supernatural resident has just visited me."

Gasps rippled through the room and eyes lingered on the wisps of cobwebs tickling Pericle's face. He couldn't have looked more convincing if he had tried.

"The ghost has informed me that today is the anniversary of his assassination, and he strongly objects to the celebration of such a joyous event as a wedding. If the ceremony goes ahead, he will curse the marriage. In view of this, I would like to speak to the bride and groom in private for a moment."

Those who had sneered at the mention of ghosts, now sneered more. Those who had arched their eyebrows now let their jaws hang, and those who had nervously looked behind now glanced at the exit.

But two people grinned from ear to hear: the bride and her mother.

***

Giulia couldn't believe her luck. The relief that flooded through her when Don Pericle interrupted the ceremony confirmed to her that she didn't want this marriage.

Now there was a chance to call off the wedding. Postponing it would give her time to talk to Riccardo, time to plan what they should tell their families and friends, and time to plan how to minimise Riccardo's humiliation. Hurting him was the last thing she wanted. It had been her fear of hurting him that had allowed things to go this far.

She glanced at Riccardo. There was confusion, irritation and reluctance on his face as they followed Don Pericle and retraced their steps down the corridor. Riccardo darted suspicious glances at the portraits on the walls, as if the pestiferous ghost might be hiding in one of them.

Don Pericle stopped outside his study. "I don't want you to influence each other when I ask you what you want to do, so I will ask you separately. Ladies first. Riccardo, please, wait here."

Riccardo's brow knotted, but he obediently sat down on the red velvet armchair in the antechamber.

Giulia found it strange to be in the green study again. It was here that Don Pericle had received them on that first meeting, here that they had planned every aspect of the ceremony and the party, and here that she finally had the opportunity to undo it all. The whole messed-up affair would come full circle if she didn't waste her chance this time.

Don Pericle closed the door behind them and looked into her eyes knowingly. For the first time in months, Giulia felt safe to speak the truth.

"I don't want to marry Riccardo."

"That's a relief, because I made up the story of the ghost."

"Oh, thank you, Don Pericle!" She laid her hands on her heart.

"You mustn't thank me. You

must thank your mother. She guessed that you weren't happy, the way a mother can. You have been lucky. Sometimes upsetting a man is the kindest, most loving thing you can do to him."

Giulia nodded, blinking back a tear.

"Now, do you want me to tell Riccardo, or will you tell him yourself?"

It was the last thing she wanted to do, but it was her duty. "I will."

***

Don Pericle left Giulia and Riccardo in his study to have the talk that they should have had much earlier, and returned to the ballroom.

It would be a pity to send the guests home, and all the food for the wedding lunch was ready anyway, so he announced that the wedding had been postponed, but the party reception would go ahead immediately. Then he instructed the waiters to serve the aperitifs.

As soon as the alcohol got flowing, the ghost stories that went round the hall became wilder and wilder.

***

Giulia and Riccardo eventually got married, but not to each other.

Don Pericle heard about it years later and wasn't surprised. He knew that Giulia ultimately wanted a marriage because she had told him '*I don't want to marry Riccardo*', not '*I don't want to get married*'.

The reason for their break-up was officially attributed to the ghost who, apparently, had been so displeased about the wedding that he had cursed the couple, despite the cancellation. This meant that nobody troubled Giulia or Riccardo with questions on the whys and hows of their break-up, because everyone knew that there was nothing logical in ghosts' behaviours.

Instead, the extra questions came to Don Pericle. From that non-wedding onwards, before setting a date for their wedding, his clients would invariably ask him to clear it first with the ghost.

8. WORKING TOGETHER

Melina didn't like teamwork. Especially when it involved her husband against his will.

It wasn't that she didn't love him—far from it: she loved him more than she loved their dog, Bellissimo. She just strongly believed that if you want something done well, you should do it yourself.

Things never went well when they had to work together. It had happened with the choice of the sofa, which she didn't much like; with the ballroom dancing classes, which they had to give up; and with the gymnastics for couples, which they never signed up for. But this was different: she desperately wanted to do it.

"Father Pietro would like us to help out at the marriage preparation courses in the parish," she told Tanino as breezily as she could, after dinner. He was always better disposed with a full tummy.

He raised a suspicious eyebrow and briefly glanced away from the Telegiornale TV news blaring in the kitchen. "Father Pietro is really scraping the bottom of the barrel."

Melina felt a little prick of offence but then supposed that Tanino didn't mean that both of them were the bottom of the barrel, only him.

"Why doesn't Father ask Vincenzo and Anna? He buys her flowers every week," Tanino continued.

He didn't sound sarcastic, which confused Melina a bit.

"They must be busy," she answered candidly.

"There must be thousands of better couples than us in Palermo. Surely hundreds just in our parish."

"Maybe they don't want to do it."

"I wonder why," he said.

This time his voice was sarcastic.

"Tanino, it's an enormous honour to be asked. And I want to say yes."

Tanino groaned, dropped the remote control and ran a hand over his face. "And everyone knows what happens when you want something, my Melina."

***

"You're going to make us late, Tanino!" his wife called from the door of their flat. "Why didn't you go to the bathroom earlier?"

Tanino tried to suppress the urge to shout back that he didn't need it earlier. Why did Melina have a habit of shouting from the door? The stairwell was so echoey that every soul in their block of flats would now be aware that he was in the loo. Then Bellissimo barked. Great. That would be the last straw to infuriate the neighbours. They would soon be called nuisance residents, if they weren't already.

"Hurry up, Tanino!"

"Go on your own. I can't come. I'm feeling unwell," he finally shouted back.

He heard the click-clacking of her heels approaching down the corridor, stopping behind the door.

"Are you joking? I'd make a terrible impression if I turn up on my own to talk about how to have a good marriage!"

Tanino reflected for a moment and had to admit that she had a point.

"If you're that unwell, you'll have *pastina in bianco* tomorrow," she said.

Tiny pasta dressed just with olive oil was the food for upset stomachs, and Tanino hated it. Melina knew that and was clearly testing him, but he was past caring about food.

"I'm so unwell that I don't want any food for one week," he answered.

"Then we can't go. I'm calling Father and cancelling," she said, without trying to disguise the annoyance in her voice.

The news of the cancellation had a miraculous effect and, a few minutes later, Tanino emerged from the bathroom like new.

"I feel much better!"

"Great. Then put on your coat. We're going."

"What? I thought you had cancelled."

"Father Pietro pointed out that I had got the time wrong: the session starts at half-past-eight, so we are still in time."

This time Tanino found himself inside the lift before he had time to get tummy ache.

***

The meeting room was on the top floor of the church annex. Tanino didn't trust lifts in buildings which were older than his own, and Melina didn't think it appropriate to go separate ways on this occasion, so she had no choice but to slog up the stairs with him.

By the time they had reached the door of the meeting room, she was out of breath and her blouse stuck uncomfortably to her skin. This was already enough to put her in a bad mood.

"Wait," she gasped out as her husband reached for the door handle. She wanted to catch her breath before making their entry. Ideally, she would have also checked her hair in a mirror, but she knew that there were no mirrors in the building.

Tanino didn't seem to hear her, and opened the door.

Suddenly Melina was faced with a room full of people, all sitting around a table. She felt exposed, like an earthworm pulled out of the soil.

She squirmed through the door, twisting her skirt to realign the seams with her hips. This was not the dignified entry she had planned, and she felt a prick of irritation.

When her husband sat down on an empty chair without any free seats next to it, leaving her standing, she became more than a little peeved.

Father Pietro's voice came from the other side of the round table. "Come and sit here, both of you." He smiled, patting two empty seats next to him.

"Tanino and Melina are our special guests tonight," the priest announced to the six young couples.

A special guest! Melina flounced to her seat.

"They know more about married life than I do," Father continued.

Melina felt her chest swell. Having studied little and always worked in the home, sometimes she felt that everyone else had a special skill, except her. But now, after fifty years, she was a 'marriage expert'—how wonderful!

"What do you think is the secret to a happy and lasting marriage?" Father asked.

Melina opened her mouth to speak but Tanino beat her to it.

"Forgiveness. That's the absolute key," he declared solemnly, and everyone nodded approvingly.

Melina now felt even more uneasy than before: why would

Tanino say such a thing, when everyone would think that she was a terrible wife and he had to forgive her many misdeeds?

"Forgiveness is nothing," she contradicted him. "The only important thing in a marriage is hard work. When the other person comes home expecting dinner, whether you've had a good or a bad day, whether you're going down with a cold, or been so busy with the children that you haven't had time to shop, let alone cook, then marriage is really hard w—"

"I've never demanded that you cook when you're unwell," Tanino objected.

"Oh, yes, you have," Melina insisted.

"No! I always buy a pizza from the baker when you're down with a cold or flu."

"Only when I'm down with something catching. When my legs play up, you still expect me to cook," Melina said.

"But your legs 'play up' every night!" Tanino protested.

"You see?"

He ran a hand over his face. She had won.

"But I've forgiven you," she announced magnanimously.

"So now you're admitting that forgiveness is more important than hard work!" Tanino jumped at his chance.

"No, I'm not. I'm only saying that forgiveness is hard work," she retorted.

"Yes, and it's especially hard work when your wife is being contrary." Tanino winked at the other men.

That conspiratorial gesture was the last straw, and Melina saw red.

How dare he make her look ridiculous like that? Anger pricked the back of her eyes. She had to leave the room.

"Excuse me, I need the bathroom," she said, and dived for the door.

***

Melina should have gone to the toilet before leaving the house, Tanino thought. Well, at least now he could enjoy a few minutes without her.

When she was in that contrary mood he couldn't bear her. He also didn't like the way she lorded it over him when they were in the parish. The fact that he only went to church on Sunday, while she went every day and was on the cleaning roster, didn't mean that it wasn't his church too! And so was the marriage. Father Pietro had invited both to speak.

For that same reason, he didn't feel that he should continue the session without Melina, so he asked the young couples to tell him what they had done in the previous sessions.

Soon, they had run out of things to say and Melina wasn't back yet.

Now he felt sorry for her. His heart told him that he should go and offer comfort.

"If you excuse me a moment, I need to check on my wife," he said.

To his surprise, everyone agreed. He was heading for the toilets when he found her in the corridor, leaning on the wall by a window.

"My treasure, are you alright?"

She turned. Her eyes were red with tears. Oh, no! He felt like crying, too and wrapped his arms around her. "What's the matter, my love?"

"I felt like a fool. I felt that you wanted to make me look stupid. I've never been a 'special guest' before. I wanted to look good in front of the young couples." She sobbed.

"I am so sorry," Tanino said, choking on the lump in his throat. "I didn't realise. I should have been more considerate. Come, let's start again. Together. Because we are a team, aren't we?"

Melina nodded and he offered her his handkerchief. She wiped her eyes and blew her nose.

"Are my eyes red?" she asked.

There were no mirrors, not even in the toilets, so he lied. "Not at all."

She put her hand in his and he squeezed it, then they walked back.

"Are you ready?" he asked her, before opening the door.

She nodded and gave him a large smile, which he didn't quite understand.

He opened the door and they walked in together. The concern on everyone's faces turned into smiles when they saw their hands clasped together.

Father Pietro cleared his throat. "I'm scrapping the list of questions I was going to ask you, because the thing we're all dying to know is how you solve your conflicts and make peace."

Tanino smiled.

"That's easy," he said, looking at Melina. "It's simply called love."

9. THE SOUND OF STRINGS

A man can be a bachelor for many reasons. He might prefer his own company, he might not have met the right person, or he might have been too busy to notice.

He might be too shy to express his feelings to the woman he loves.

This was the case for engineer Mario Bianchi. The fifty-five-year-old lived on the outskirts of the Sicilian capital, Palermo, on the top floor of a three-storey building that he had inherited from his parents. He had his studio on the ground floor and he let the middle floor to a concert violinist, Anna Neri.

They had met fewer times than he could count on two hands—mostly passing on the stairs—but Mario felt that he knew his tenant and neighbour very well. From nine till five, while he sat in his studio doing calculations and making plans on his computer, he could hear her practise the music that she would play in the theatre in the evening.

The notes that filtered through the floors told him a lot about her. She was full of passion and emotion, but she was also steadfast and determined. She never let a crocked note slip without repeating the bar, and she practised eight hours a day, including weekends.

She must be a fine violinist because her music had taken his heart to a wonderful place, where it had never been before: a place called 'in love'.

Mario couldn't tell her about his feelings. He could explain at length tensile stress, axial loads and modulus of rupture, but he couldn't talk about love. So when he crossed her on the stairs one day, the best he could do was to use their surnames—Bianchi (white) and Neri (black)—as a metaphor.

"When white and black mix together, they make my favourite colour. Grey," he told her.

She didn't seem to catch his subtle allusion.

"My favourite colour is blue," she replied.

That attempt had failed, so he gathered his courage again. "Did you know that our flats were originally joined together into one home?" he asked the next time he met her. "Wouldn't it be nice to reunite them?"

"Are you saying that you want to join the flats into one?" she asked, looking a little worried.

"Yes," he said.

"When?"

"As soon as possible."

Now she looked very worried. Mario had prepared for her to react with happiness, sympathy, indignation or even indifference. But not with worry.

***

Time was not on her side, Anna thought. Between her landlord's threat to evict her to join the two flats, and her biological clock ticking loudly now that her fortieth birthday had come, time was not her friend.

Having devoted her life to music, she had never taken time to find a man and start a family. But today, on her fortieth birthday, the alarm clock was ringing and there was no violin music that could drown the racket.

She put on a quick wash, had breakfast and checked her phone. There were a few birthday messages from family and friends, but she was too old for presents. At least, that was what her family must have thought.

She pulled her wet washing out

of the machine and hung it on the balcony's lines to dry. Unfortunately, one of her favourite stockings slipped between her fingers and landed on the pavement below.

***

Peppino, the travelling greengrocer, sang in Sicilian dialect in his deep baritone voice to announce to the street's residents that he had arrived with his tomatoes and artichokes.

Right on cue, his loyal customer, the engineer that lived on the top floor, peeked out from his balcony.

"Peppino, I'd like half a kilo of tomatoes and four artichokes," he called, lowering his wicker basket with a rope.

Peppino wrapped a sheet of grey paper around his fist to make a cone and filled it with tomatoes, then took the money from the basket and put the cone in, together with the artichokes.

He was about to tell the man that he could pull the basket up when a flash of white on the pavement caught his eye.

It was a lacy white stocking. It must have fallen from the washing lines of the middle floor. Peppino was about to shout up to the woman who was hanging her washing when she disappeared inside.

If he put that stocking in his customer's basket, the man could take it to his neighbour—it was better than leaving it on the pavement.

Peppino placed the stocking in the basket with the tomatoes and artichokes and shouted to his customer. "Served! You can pull up!"

Then he continued cruising down the street, singing about his artichokes without thorns and his tomatoes ripe and sweet.

***

When Mario inspected his basket, he got a shock. He had no doubt who the owner of that stocking was, and that she had put it into his basket deliberately.

If the garment had caught in the wicker as the basket travelled up, it would have been hanging off the side, damaged. But it was neatly folded between the tomatoes and the artichokes.

What could be the meaning of that gesture? Was she trying to tell him that she had decided to accept his marriage proposal? The mere possibility made him flush and shiver all at once.

Later that morning, for the first time in years, Mario closed his studio during working hours. He went to the barber to get a haircut, bought a new suit and purchased a huge bunch of red roses. Then he knocked on her door.

The sound of the violin immediately stopped and he heard her steps approaching the door.

"Hello," she greeted him. As soon as her gaze landed on the roses, she smiled up to her eyes. "A present for my birthday! How did you know?"

This time he didn't trust himself to say a word—words had failed him in the past. He just smiled and offered her the roses.

"Come in," she said. "Can I offer you a coffee?"

He nodded, even though caffeine was the last thing his galloping heart needed.

Later that day she brought him a piece of cake, and the following day, when he went down to return her plate, she invited him for another coffee.

At that point he felt brave enough to tell her how much he enjoyed hearing her play, so she played for him for two hours.

They went for a walk to buy ingredients for lunch, which they cooked together, as cooking for two was more fun than cooking for one. While they were cooking, they happened to chat about how convenient it would have been if the flats had still been joined by an internal stair, like they were in the past. At that, he told her that he loved her and wished to marry her. She said yes.

It was only on the day of their wedding that he remembered to return the stocking to her, and asked her to wear it under her dress for good luck.

Many happy years of married life

went by, but Anna never asked Mario where or how he got her stocking...

10. NOT JUST A PRETTY FACE

Ash Wednesday was the one day in the year when Melina wished she had a fringe.

Why was Father Pietro always so generous with the ashes he put on her forehead? It was easy for him. The presbytery was attached to the church and he didn't have to walk the streets of Palermo to get home.

But this year Melina had come prepared: with a woollen hat. She was about to pull it down on her head and step out of the church when Peppina stopped her.

"Hello, darling. Isn't it a little too warm for a hat?" her friend asked.

She had a point. It was one of those Sicilian February days when spring seems to have arrived in full swing.

"I do feel the cold," Melina lied.

Peppina narrowed her eyes. "It's because you're embarrassed about the ashes on your forehead, isn't it? You shouldn't be. It's silly. What do looks matter, anyway? Intelligence is much more important."

It was easy for Peppina to say that. She had studied and had been a teacher and even a headmistress. Melina, on the contrary, had barely finished primary school and had never held a job. Even now that she was well past retirement age, her lack of education and professional accomplishments still stung. Why shouldn't she cling to the only thing she had ever had—her looks?

No, she did not want to walk home looking like a chimney sweep, thank you very much. She pulled her hat down and, without replying to Peppina, set off home.

***

Ash Wednesday was a day of fasting and penance, so lunch was only bread and water, which didn't help put Melina back in a good mood. She ate with her husband, in silence, watching the one o'clock news.

Was it a coincidence that today all the journalists were good-looking women? The foreign correspondent, a pretty woman with intelligent eyes, fearlessly interviewed a mob of protesters.

Next came an interview with the chair of the International Monetary Fund, an elegant middle-aged woman, followed by the German chancellor—also a woman—addressing her country with a look of intelligent determination.

Melina sighed and put down her hunk of bread. She had lost her appetite. How was it that every woman in the world was cleverer and more capable than her?

Maybe she was clever and capable, too, but in her own realm: at home.

Peppina had told her about a foreign dish called lentil curry, which would be perfect for the Fridays of Lent. Melina decided that she would prove her worth with this new adventurous dish.

First thing the next morning, Melina rushed to the supermarket. Usually she walked straight past the foreign food section, but this time, she stopped and perused the shelves.

She had never tasted coconut milk or ground coriander, and the only thing she knew about cumin was that the Pharisees in the Gospel paid the tithe for it, and Jesus told them off for it.

There it was: a sachet called 'curry'. She picked it up and read the instructions on the back. The recipe was precisely for lentil curry, but unfortunately, all the amounts were in ounces and pints. Oh, dear. She had no idea how to convert them into grams and litres. Of course, Peppina could, with all her qualifications and brains! Suddenly, Melina didn't feel like a capable and adventurous woman anymore.

She put the sachet back on the shelf and left the supermarket, feeling very small. Lunch would have to be pasta with tomato sauce.

She strode purposefully to the greengrocer but, when she got there, there were two kinds of tomatoes for sale. The loose tomatoes sold at two euros per kilo, while the bags of ten went for one euro seventy-five. Which was cheaper? She turned the numbers in her head but couldn't come to a solution.

"How can I help?" the greengrocer asked her.

Oh, dear, she had wasted her time trying impossible calculations and still hadn't decided. She shot a panicked glance at the other vegetables. The peppers were clearly marked and there was no choice. A simple purchase for a simple woman.

"I'll have three peppers, please," she said, defeated.

Lunch would have to be pasta with roasted peppers.

***

"*Nonna*, how can I remember all these dates? It's impossible!"

Valentina protested, squirming on her chair.

Usually Tanino helped their granddaughter with her homework, but today he wasn't home.

Melina put on her glasses and sat down next to Valentina. "Let's see." She squinted at the history textbook.

Oh, no. The French Revolution. The only thing she remembered about it was that Marie Antoniette was very beautiful.

Valentina lolled her head. "How did you remember these dates when you were at school, Nonna?"

The truth was, she didn't, and she had often ended up in the corner with the 'dunce' hat on. The memory brought a shiver, and she pushed it out of her mind.

"Let's see what we can do. What does 1789 look like?"

"I don't know."

"When I look at it, I see number one like a walking stick. Number seven is a man holding that stick. Number eight is, of course, a woman, and she's holding a helium balloon which is number nine."

Melina smiled, satisfied with her mental picture, but her granddaughter was looking at her as if she had gone crazy.

"Of, course, I was only joking. There's no way to remember these numbers other than memorising them," she hurried to say.

***

The condominium residents' meetings were some of the most boring things ever. Why did her husband insist on her going with him? She never contributed to the discussion—she left that to the clever people, all the lawyers, doctors and teachers.

"What's on tonight's agenda?" Melina asked her husband.

"The school next door has lodged a complaint," Tanino replied. "They believe someone from our building is throwing bags of food to the cats and littering their property."

When they walked into the room, the meeting had started and was already animated.

"The bags can't have been thrown from our building. Only an Olympic athlete could throw as far as the far side of the school's garden," the lawyer who lived on the top floor said.

"Ah, but it depends on the height from which the bags have been thrown. It's perfectly possible from one of the higher floors," the physics professor who lived on the first floor countered.

"You are incriminating the higher floors without proof!" the lawyer retorted.

The discussion heated up, with the physics professor talking about trajectory and momentum, and the lawyer about defamation.

Melina could see a very simple solution, but if all those clever people hadn't worked it out yet, it must be wrong.

She kept quiet, but when people started getting puce in the face, she couldn't hold it any longer. She stood up. "Excuse me."

Silence descended abruptly.

"Was it you? Did you throw the bags?" the lawyer asked.

"No. I just thought that the cats might have dragged the bags of food to somewhere more convenient for them. So the place where the bags were found in the morning isn't necessarily where they originally landed."

"Valid point!" the lawyer said.

"Which means that they could have been thrown from any floor," Melina continued. "And do we know what's inside the bags? The supermarket can probably tell us who's bought what, and from that we can find out the culprit."

At that, the man from the second floor stood up and owned up. He had felt sorry for the kittens but hadn't considered the consequences of throwing food from his balcony into someone else's property. He agreed that he would apologise to the school and ask for permission to feed the cats in a more acceptable way.

Everyone looked at Melina with admiration, and she felt a little less small. Maybe she wasn't a silly old housewife after all.

When the meeting was over and they were in the lift to their floor imagine if you hadn't come to the meeting tonight!"

**

Bolstered by the evening's success, the next morning Melina went to the supermarket and bought the curry powder.

She was going to cook the lentil curry, even if that required ringing Peppina and humbly asking for her help.

"Sorry, Melina, I don't follow the recipe because I can't convert all those strange measurements in, Tanino squeezed her hand. "Just

pints and ounces. I just taste it and see if I like it," Peppina confessed.

Melina laughed. Maybe other people weren't always as clever as she imagined them to be. She thanked Peppina and got to work, adjusting the quantities according to her taste.

That day Valentina was having lunch with them. When they sat down at the table to a plate of curried lentils each, Melina's gaze flitted between her husband and her grandchild with trepidation.

Oh, dear, what if they didn't like it? She shouldn't have tried a foreign recipe with no idea of the quantities. Did she think she was a fancy chef?

She sat still, unable to put her spoon in her mouth until Valentina and Tanino had taken their first mouthfuls.

Valentina was the first to tuck in. She swallowed with a smile and licked her lips. "Nonna, I like this dish. Do it again."

Hurrah, she had done it! "I will, my treasure."

"You are such a clever nonna. Today I was called to the front of the class and the teacher asked me about the French Revolution. I remembered the man with the stick and the woman with the balloon: 1789."

Well, maybe she was a clever and capable woman after all. But why wasn't Tanino saying anything about the lentils?

"Yes, your nonna is a very clever woman," Tanino said to Valentina, then he turned to Melina and looked at her with an expression that could only be described as admiration. "I met the lawyer in the lift lobby and he asked me to give you his compliments for what you did last night."

"Thank you," Melina said.

"And, by the way, your lentils are delicious. You're not just a pretty face, my darling."

Melina smiled. She was never going to feel ugly or stupid again.

The End

Also in this series:

A Slip of the Tongue

Fresh from the Sea

Confetti and Lemon Blossom

What's Yours is Mine

Stefania Hartley

A Slip of the
Tongue

Very Large Print
short stories

Stefania Hartley

What's Yours
is Mine

Very Large Print
short stories

Stefania Hartley

Fresh from the Sea

and other short stories

Large Print

Stefania Hartley

Confetti and Lemon Blossom

Wedding stories from Don Pericle's villa

Large Print

ABOUT THE AUTHOR

Best known as The Sicilian Mama, Stefania was born in Sicily and immediately started growing, but not very much.

She left her sunny island after falling head over heels in love with an Englishman, and now she lives in the UK with her husband and their three children.

Having finally learnt English, she's enjoying it so much that she now writes short stories and romance novels. Her short stories have been longlisted for the Mogford Prize for Food and Drink Writing, commended by the Society of Medical Authors, and won other prizes, but what she likes most is to hear from her readers. If you have enjoyed her stories, she'd love you to leave a review on Amazon or Goodreads, or contact her through her website:

www.stefaniahartley.com

Facebook: www.facebook.com/StefaniaHartley

Twitter: @TheSicilianMama

If you sign up for her newsletter: www.stefaniahartley.com/subscribe

she'll send you an exclusive free copy of her short story *Not a Speck of Dust* and let you know when she's releasing a new book.